Time to Sleep SHEEP the SHEEP!

by
MO WILLEMS

Balzer + Bray
An Imprint of HarperCollinsPublishers

Time to sleep, Sheep the Sheep!

Time to sleep, Pig the Pig!

Time to sleep,

Time to sleep, Crab the Crab!

Time to sleep,
Horse the Horse!

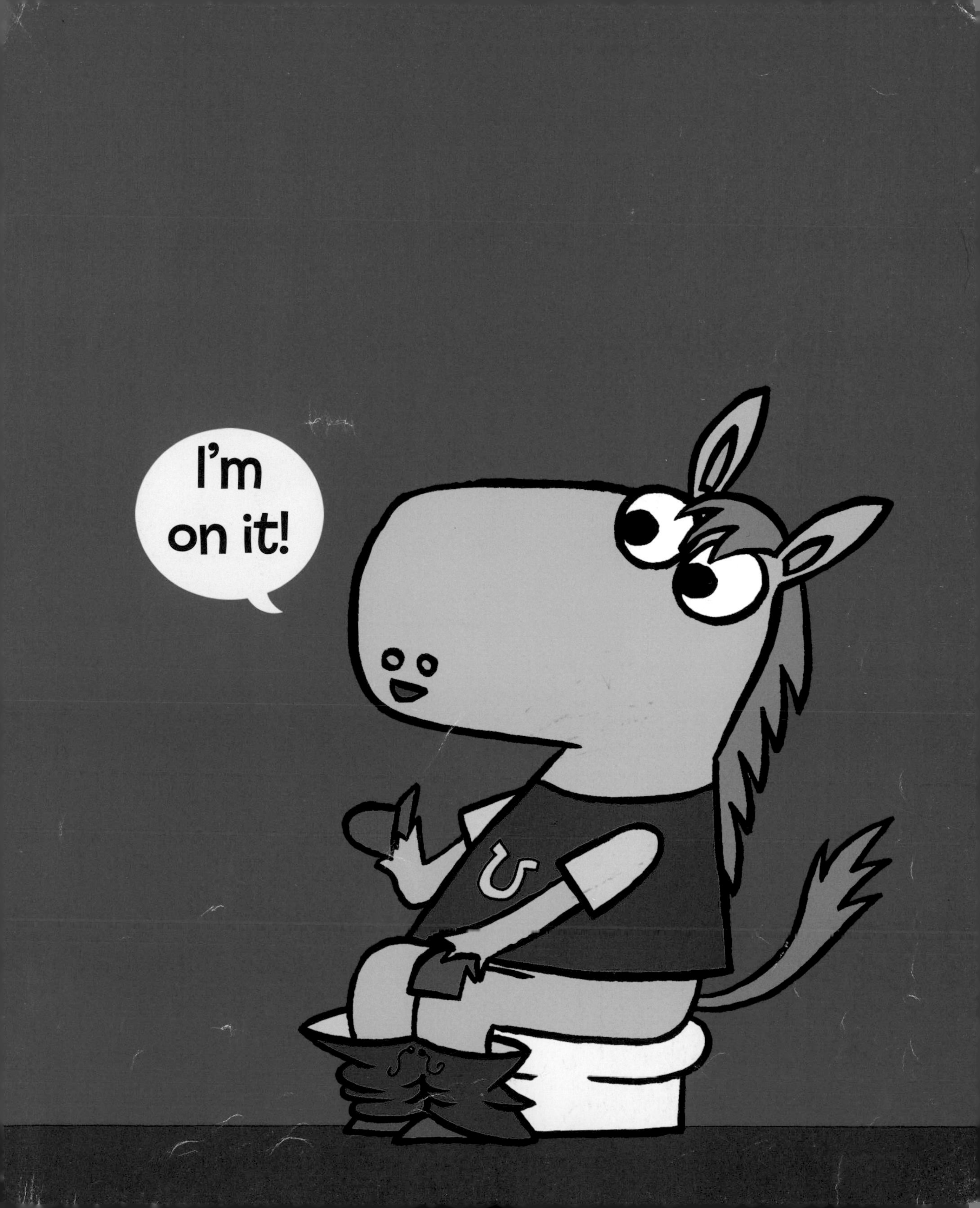
I'm on it!

Time to sleep, Shark the Shark!

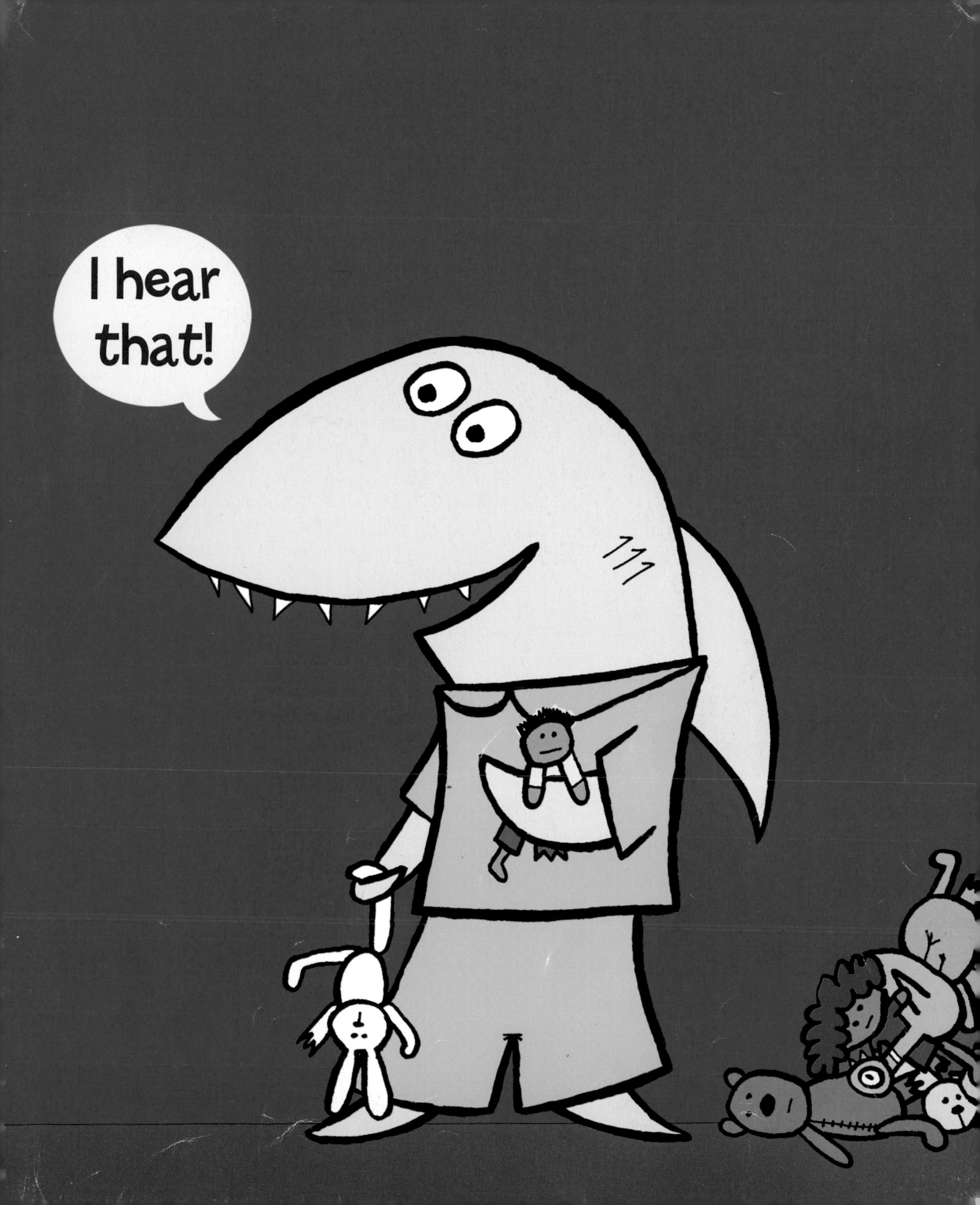
I hear that!

Time to—

To Alessandra and Martha,

who never rest until it's right

Balzer + Bray is an imprint of HarperCollins Publishers.

Time to Sleep, Sheep the Sheep!
Copyright © 2010 by Mo Willems
Printed in the U.S.A.

Library of Congress Cataloging-in-Publication Data is available.
ISBN 978-0-06-172847-1 (trade bdg.) — ISBN 978-0-06-172848-8 (lib. bdg.)

Typography by Martha Rago
10 11 12 13 14   LPR   10 9 8 7 6 5 4 3 2 1
❖
First Edition